BLACK HOLE RADIO

LABYRINTHIA

ANN BIRDGENAW

ILLUSTRATIONS BY E.M. ROBERTS

DFP

DartFrog Plus

Printed in the United States of America

ISBN: 978-1-959096-76-4 (paperback)
ISBN: 978-1-959096-77-1 (ebook)

LCCN: 2023934744

DartFrog Plus

4697 Main Street
Manchester Center, VT 05255

*I dedicate this book to my sister Dar, with love.
She inspires me every day!*

CONTENTS

CHAPTER 1

GRANDPA'S BOX

can do this! I can do this! My hands tremble as I reach for the box in the garage . . . "I *can't* do this!" I run out of the garage and throw myself onto the orange couch in 'Mission Control', our space club. I pull a pillow over my head. I've been tearing my hair out, trying to convince myself that I'm ready to go through my grandpa's boxes. After he died, my dad stored grandpa's personal things in our garage. But now dad wants to clear everything out and put the car in the garage for the winter.

What dad doesn't know is there's a black hole radio in there that's like a hyperspace highway to other planets. Matt, Celeste, and I got sucked into it by accident . . . three times! We've been to planetoid Shnergla, moon Bilaluna, and then a beautiful blue planet called Ka'Azula, where they make incredible azulizard pizza. No really, we had a pizza party, and the pizza was out of this world . . . literally!

I hear my dad's voice call out from the driveway as he leaves for work. "Hawk, don't forget to go through the boxes of Grandpa's things to keep what you want, and we'll bring the rest to the Goodwill." I slide off the couch and onto the floor. I pull out my phone. I need backup. I text Celeste:

Can you come over to UBSS like now

What up I'm reading

I was just about to go through my grandpa's stuff and . . .

OMG . . . I'm coming

Celeste is a member of our space club too, and she doesn't waste any time getting to 'Mission Control'. I hear her throw down her bicycle outside the door and burst in, panting. She looks all around, her eyes wide.

"It's okay. It's still in there." I nod my head toward the garage.

"Phew!" Celeste breathes out dramatically, dropping onto the couch next to me. "So, how do you want to do this?"

"Maybe we should carry the box in here, and if it beeps . . . we drop and run." I've been thinking about this a lot . . . but I just can't do it alone.

"Let's do it." She gets up and pulls her worry stone out of her pocket. *Rub-rub.* Celeste has Asperger's syndrome and needs her stone to help her focus.

We walk to the door connecting the club to the garage, and I slowly open the door.

"Wait!" cries Celeste making me jump back.

"What is it?" I whip around, breaking out in a sweat.

"What's that over there?" she says, pointing and rubbing her stone.

"Sheesh, Celeste, you scared me! It's just an old lamp," I tell her as we walk into the garage.

"Sorry, Hawk. I thought it was an alien. I was reading this book about scary aliens when you texted and . . ."

"I don't need to hear this now, Celeste. I'm really nervous, okay." I gulp.

She tucks her long red hair behind her ear then hands me her worry stone.

I gently take the stone and feel the soothing coolness in my palm. I flip it over in my hand, and my heartbeat slows a little. I take a breath. "Over here." I edge over to my grandpa's boxes in the corner. Careful to avoid the box with the radio, I push the box that says 'Books & Stuff – PRIVATE KEEP OUT' in my Grandpa's shaky handwriting. "This must be the one," I say.

Celeste and I each grab an end and carry it into the club. It's really heavy. We place the box on the floor, and I take a deep breath before I open it. We peer inside as if an alien is about to jump out, but it's full of the coolest stuff ever.

"Ooohhh, what's all this?" Celeste says picking up a bunch of rolled-up maps tied with string.

"Look at this," I say, pulling out a jar of rocks. "These could be moon rocks!"

I look into the depths of the box, and under the space books, I see some diaries. I pull them out and open the one on top that says 'Warning – Do Not Open – Property of Ray Bowie – June 1965 – May 70'.

I start to tear up. It's painful to read his innermost thoughts about our relationship and the secrets he kept from me. We were so close, yet he had this whole

other life that I didn't know about. I open a random page and see my Grandpa's familiar handwriting. I read . . .

Russ is coming over tonight to watch 'The Twilight Zone.' I really want to tell him my great big secret. It's so hard to keep this great big secret to myself. It's like I'm living in a twilight zone.

I skip a bunch of pages and read another passage:

Maggie is so fun at school, and she's even into space stuff. I wonder what she thinks about wormholes? I'll recommend the book 'A Wrinkle in Time' to her tomorrow and see if she likes it . . . or believes it can actually happen.

I shuffle the journals around and find the one I'm looking for—the last journal before he died, dated June 2016 - June 2021. I start to open it, and then I hand it over to Celeste, "Here, can you read the passages at the end for me? I . . . I can't do it."

"Sure, Hawk." She takes the journal from me and opens it up to a random page, looks at me, and starts to read . . .

Hawk came over with his folks today. I told him about exoplanets, and we talked about going camping to watch the Perseid meteor shower. The lad is growing up so fast. I have to tell him about the radio next time we go camping.

She flips some pages, then a few more, and reads . . .

It's so important to let him know about the radio. We'll go planet-hopping together for the first few times, and he'll see that it's better to take the radio with you through the wormhole to make it easier to get back home . . .

She stops reading and looks up at me, blinking. We are reading each other's minds.

Take the radio with us! OMG, why didn't we think of that?

CHAPTER 2

A PAIN IN THE BRAIN

I'm so distracted in science class. I keep thinking about the wonderful things I've been reading in my grandpa's journals. Grandpa was like a cosmic Indiana Jones or something! My mind starts to wander as I picture him in a brown fedora, expertly cracking his whip to fight off the bad aliens. Then he saves the pretty girl alien as they swing together across the chasm on his whip. My eyes close as I imagine I'm wearing the fedora, and I'm rescuing Celeste from the evil Pixies of Polaris. A smile spreads across my face as we swing across the galactic landscape on a bullwhip. Yippee-ka-y . . .

I'm jolted back to the present when I hear my name. Mr. Brainer is calling out the names of the 'science buddy' teams. My eyes pop open. Wait. What?

"Earth calling Hawk. Hawk, I said you're with Mikey . . ." Mr. Brainer fixes me with a stare before continuing to call out the teams.

I'm wide awake now. How did this happen? I'm stuck with Big Mikey as my 'science buddy' for the end-of-year science fair project. Mr. Brainer said something about exploring science, inventions, and friendships. Great! I have to be 'buddies' with the school bully. At least he was nice last month when Matt slam-dunked his rebound to win the basketball game.

"Looks like I lucked out this time!" Big Mikey's voice booms out across the science lab. "I'm with space-boy, Stephen *Hawking*!"

Oh, brother! This is going to be fun! And by fun, I mean no fun at all!

"Hey, Big Mikey . . . errr Mikey," I stammer nervously as he approaches my table. "Yeah, this is great!"

"So . . ." he says, looking at me expectantly.

"So . . ." This will be like pulling teeth, I think. "What should we do for the project?" I ask him.

"I don't know. You're supposed to know." He snaps, sitting down next to me because Mr. Brainer wants us to brainstorm topics for the project.

"Do you want to do the volcano thing?" I ask him.

"No, I did that already. Don't you have any original ideas?" He stares at me and curls his lip, daring me to argue.

Ugh. "How about magnets?" I ask.

"Too easy,"

"Worms?" I offer.

"Too slimy."

"Clouds?" I say.

"Boring!" he says, getting bored.

I am wracking my brain now. "What about popcorn?"

His head pops up. "Like, how do you eat it? I like mine with butter."

I think we're getting somewhere. "More like, how do you make it? What does it take to pop a kernel of corn?"

Mikey looks hungry. "Then can we eat it?"

"Uh, sure," I reply, eager to find a topic and end this painful conversation.

I'm with Space boy!

Mikey is eager to get to the part where we eat the popcorn. "Okay, so now what?"

"Um, well, we should write all this down," I say, looking at him, hoping he'll pull out some paper, but he just sits there looking at me.

Yup, this is going to be fun. I look over at Matt's workstation to see that his partner is Celeste. How did he get so lucky?!

Big Mikey suddenly looks inspired, and I start to think that maybe this will be okay when he says, smiling, "Why don't you invite me over to your 'space club' after school so we can work on it?"

CHAPTER 3

PRACTICE MAKES PERFECT

After school, I meet up with Celeste and Matt, who are supercharged about making the basketball playoffs. They don't notice how quiet I am.

"Celeste, with you and me on the team, we can go all the way! We've won five games in a row, and I'm sure we'll make the playoffs," Matt crows.

Celeste nods. "Yeah, it's great that everyone on the team shares in the scoring. I only score a few last-minute baskets when the games are close."

"With a little help from you, Stretch has the most offensive rebounds in the league," Matt continues.

"And Beaner has the most blocked shots," Celeste adds.

"And I can hit the same spot on the backboard, so my hook shots always fall in." I add to the conversation.

I am distracted about Big Mikey coming to 'Mission Control', but it's true; our team is improving, even without Celeste's help. Stretch has learned how to out-position the other forwards and centers, so he gets almost all the rebounds. Stretch, Matt and Beaner are jumping higher every game, so Celeste helps them less and less. We have an amazing fast break, where I get ESP'd when Beaner is going to block a shot as I get near him to pick up the loose ball. I throw it first to Big Mikey, who then sets up an alley-oop for

Stretch. Celeste helped the first few times, but after a few games, she stopped helping us. I couldn't believe it when Beaner blocked a shot, and Mikey set up Matt, who did a lay-up all on his own.

Celeste and I practice with Mouse, who got his nickname because he's the smallest on the team. Coach Soggybottom said he picked him for the team because of his hustle and never-quit attitude. Before Celeste and I joined the team, Mouse was always on the bench and never got to play during games. But during practice, he worked harder than anyone. If the team bogged down in practice, the coach would say, "You guys are so slow. You can't even catch a mouse," as Mouse ran circles around us. After one practice, Celeste and I approached Mouse. He was still shooting baskets from the foul line, as he did after every practice. He had a great shooting technique and sunk nine out of ten foul shots most days.

"Mouse, because you're short, you need to shoot from further out, so there's no one to block your shot," I tell him.

He had no confidence. "I know, but I can't reach the basket when I shoot from further out; they're all air balls."

Celeste encouraged him, "You've been practicing your shot so much that I'm sure if you backed up just a little every day, you could do it. Why don't you try backing up one step and see how it goes?"

"Okay, I'll try." He took a step back from the foul line and shot the ball. It was right on a perfect line but was about a foot short. "See what I mean? Air balls!" wailed Mouse.

"Try again. You just need to figure out the range. Right, Celeste?" I said, giving her a knowing smile.

"Okay, but I'll just miss again. I don't have the arm power like you guys." He took the shot, and Celeste pushed it a little with her telekinesis, so it ticked the inside of the rim and fell into the basket.

"You did it, see!" I shout high-fiving both of them. He took five more shots, and they all went straight in—swish.

"Try backing up another step tomorrow and see how you do," Celeste says.

For the next half-dozen practices, Celeste and I encouraged Mouse to back up a step further every day until he got beyond the 3-point line. For the first few weeks, he needed a little boost from Celeste for shots more than sixteen feet, but soon, he was deadly accurate for all his shots. When Coach Soggybottom saw his outside shooting, he let him play in the games. Before long, Mouse was making three-pointers half the time, all on his own.

"Hey Hawk, why so quiet?" Celeste and Matt stop walking and look at me questioningly.

"I have something to tell you. Big Mikey is coming to the clubhouse today."

CHAPTER 4

THE FIRST RULE OF SPACE CLUB

"What? No way, Hawk!" Matt says.

Celeste just stares at me and rubs her worry stone.

"How could I say no?" I tell them what happened in science class. "Mikey caught me off guard!"

"But, Big Mikey—in 'Mission Control'? This is not good, Hawk! Not Good!" Matt says as we walk again.

"Yeah, it's our 'space' for space," adds Celeste, looking away.

"I know, but I really want to do well on this project. Mr. Brainer said it's for twenty-five percent of our grade . . . besides, it'll just be for an hour," I try to reassure them. "So, come over at six o'clock, and we'll have pizza and watch the new episode of 'Star Trekkers' like usual."

"Okay, Hawk, but if he goes into the garage, slam the door and run for your life!" Matt says with raised eyebrows.

"Ha-ha! Funny, Matt! Do you think I'd let him go anywhere near that radio?" I laugh, trying to keep my voice from shaking.

Celeste gulps. "No, but what if it beeps while he's there?"

I hadn't thought of that.

We look at each other with big round eyes, imagining Big Mikey bullying his way into the garage and picking up the glowing radio. Big Mikey is the last person we want to know our little secret. We have a portal to other planets in my garage. He'll call us space-weirdos, and he'll get angry if he learns about our superpowers. We don't want him to know that we have ESP, a gift from the Supreme Leader of Shnergla. We used our ESP last month to get Mikey to stop bullying kids at school. Come to think of it, he's been a lot nicer to everyone since we discovered he has a secret: he doesn't know who his father is. I kind of feel sorry for him, but maybe that's why he's so mean all the time.

I arrive home and rush into 'Mission Control' to put away all our secret space stuff and get ready before Big Mikey shows up.

I hear a knock and open the door to Big Mikey. He enters slowly, looking all around. Like he's always wondered what goes on in here. There's an old computer, lots of posters of planets, buttons and knobs on the wall, and glow-in-the-dark stars on the ceiling for a cool effect at night. There's even a real telescope my grandpa gave me for scanning the cosmos for UFOs.

"Come sit down Bi . . . errr Mikey. We can work over here," I say, feeling self-conscious and eager to get this over with.

"Hey, this is lit! What's the name of your club?" he asks.

"We call it the UBSS, 'Uranus is the Butt of the Solar System,'" I answer, relaxing a little.

"Ha-ha, that's gucci!" he says, sitting down on our old orange couch.

"Okay, so I thought we could make a research plan and think of some questions that may lead to a popcorn experiment," I tell him, getting right to the project.

"Yeah, sounds good," he replies, still checking out the clubhouse.

"What do you think about popcorn?" I ask him.

"Ummmm, I know! Why does it cost so much for a little box of popped corn at the movies?" Mikey points at me like this is the number one question about popcorn.

"Okay, I'll write that one down. Anything else? Maybe something more . . . scientific?" I add, trying to steer him in the right direction.

He pauses, "Why does burnt popcorn smell so awful? I hate that when I burn it in the microwave." We look at each other as the conversation trails off.

"Alright, we can put that down, too. How about what makes popcorn pop?" I say, getting into it.

Mikey points at the paper. "Oh, I just thought of something wicked cool: can the hot sun turn corn-on-the-cob into popped corn-on-the-cob?" Mikey says, getting excited, "write that down, Hawk!"

"Oh yeah, that's a good one," I tell him, writing like mad. "Are there different kernels you can use for popping?" I add to the growing list of questions.

"Okay, that's enough. What do we do now?" Big Mikey asks, and I roll my eyes and groan inwardly. Who does he think I am? Stephen Hawking, the famous cosmologist I'm named after?

"Let's do some research on the computer for fun popcorn experiments," I offer, walking towards the old

desktop computer in our club. "We can find the mate-
rials we need."

"Yeah, yeah. Let's do that," Mikey says, following
me. "I never knew science could be fu . . ."

Beep, beep, beep, beep! Four beeps and a pause
came from the garage. I stop in my tracks.

"What's that beeping sound?" he asks, looking
around.

"I didn't hear anything," I lie, backing up towards
the exit. "L-let's go to my house for some, some corn,"
I stammer, opening the door. "We'll see how long they
take to pop in the microwave."

Beep, beep, beep, beep!

"Wait, Hawk. I just heard it again." He holds up a
finger and looks around. He's getting more curious
and heads toward the door connected to the garage.
"I think it came from over here."

"Oh, that! That's nothing. Just an old alarm clock
in my dad's garage. It's defective. Let's go make some
popcorn," I say, stepping through the doorway.

Beep, beep, beep, beep! The sound is much louder
as Mikey opens the door. I catch a green glow out of
the corner of my eye and run as fast as I can to my
house.

CHAPTER 5

MAYDAY, MAYDAY!

I text Matt and Celeste to meet up at my place right away for an emergency 'Club' meeting. Pacing in my room, I wait for them to arrive. Matt and Celeste rush up to my room, and I fill them in on what happened.

"We were in 'Mission Control' working on our project when the beeping started," I say.

"What?" Matt and Celeste cry. "No way!" They look at each other in shock, and Matt does a face palm.

"What did you do?" Matt asks.

"I did what you told me to do—I ran!" I say, feeling a little ashamed. "He wouldn't let it go."

"Let's not panic. Let's go back to the clubhouse. He may still be in there," says Celeste calmly.

"Okay, let's go," I say, sounding braver than I feel.

My mom pops her head out of the kitchen as we head down the stairs. "How many friends for pizza tonight, Hawk?" she asks as we all freeze, and no one says anything.

"Ummm, I'll ask and let you know, mom," I fumble to answer.

"Sure, honey. Did you get Grandpa's boxes out of the garage yet?"

"Yup," I answer, eager to avoid going into detail. Celeste and I hid the box with the radio in a small cupboard in the garage. Right now, we have bigger things to worry about—like where in the universe is Big Mikey? We leave the safety of the house and creep over to the clubhouse. We look in the window and don't see any sign of Big Mikey anywhere.

"Open the door, Hawk," says Matt, hiding behind me.

"You open it!" I say, pushing him in front of me.

"No . . . you," he starts to say as Celeste steps forward and slowly opens the door.

We look at each other and follow her inside. There's no sign of Mikey or any beeping from the garage, either.

"Well, that's it! The radio got him. He's probably on some faraway planet right now, wondering what the heck happened," Matt says sadly. "Oh well, let's go back in the house and watch the 'Star Trekkers'," he says, immediately cheering up.

"Wait, Matt! We can't let Mikey go through the wormhole by himself. He'd never survive. We have to go after him to help him get back safely," I say, looking from one to the other to see their reactions.

"Oh, no! No way, Hawk. I don't need to go through that space-warp tunnel again. Look what happened last time." Matt says, vigorously shaking his awesome afro for effect. "You guys turned blue, and I almost had to eat worms!"

I look at Celeste to see she's thinking about the consequences of another trip down the hyperspace highway.

"I don't know, Hawk. But I know that Mikey needs help to get back to Earth. Can we live with him

disappearing, never to be seen again?" she says, looking at each of us.

"You're right, Celeste. We'd never have to deal with
Big Mikey's bullying again!" Matt shrugs sheepishly.

"That's why we have to save him. Or we'll never for-
give ourselves for being selfish," she says, looking from
Matt to me.

"Maybe this can help us," I pull the notebook out
of my back pocket. "I found this with my grandpa's
things."

They read the cover: *Hawk's Handbook.*

"I haven't read all of it yet. I wanted to read it with
you guys. This tells us everything we need to know
about the black hole radio; how it works, how to set it
with the tuner, and importantly, how to use it to get
back to Earth." *Thank you, Grandpa!* "Maybe we can
find something to help us get Mikey back?"

Celeste and Matt crowd around me, jostling to read
my grandpa's scratchy handwriting.

"This is going to be great!" chuckles Matt. "Now we
can listen to *Rocket Man* on the radio as we beam to
other planets," he jokes.

"It says here that we can use the radio tuner to go
to a different place by turning the dial and waiting for
a beep." Celeste reads. "If we turn the dial back again
to where it was, we'll go to the same planet as Mikey.
Oh, and look here—the beeping sound means the radio
is in **transmit mode**. Push the tiny button on the left
side of the radio to disconnect it. He even drew a little
diagram of the radio and what the buttons mean." We
lean in to look at all the notes on the drawing.

"Transmit mode! No wonder we've been getting sucked in." I slap my forehead. "We'll have to learn all this stuff when we get back from rescuing Mikey." I look around at my friends, waiting for their agreement.

"But where can we put the radio to bring it with us?" Matt asks.

Celeste and I look at each other as we turn Matt around, and I gently slide the radio into his backpack.

"What? Not my backpack! I don't want to . . ." Before Matt can complain, Celeste reaches in and turns the tuner dial one way and then back until the familiar beeping starts.

CHAPTER 6

CAN SOMEONE TURN ON THE LIGHTS?

We tumble head over foot in zero gravity through a tunnel that stretches and shrinks, tilts and straightens, as brilliant beams from cool flames flash by us at light speed, illuminating the darkness around us as we sink into unconsciousness.

I wake up, but I feel sleepy because it's pitch dark all around me. It smells dank and musty, like an old basement or . . . or a wet dog. I feel something soft lick my cheek, and I wake right up.

"Matt, Celeste, help! Are you here?" I croak, nearly a whisper. I hear some panting and that soft lick on my face again. *What the . . .*

"Okay, who's there?" I ask, sitting up. I remember that I still have my cell phone in my back pocket. Pulling it out, I flick on the flashlight app and immediately let out a screech! "Aaahhhh!" There's a big alien tiger right in front of me, with its tongue hanging out like it's about to chomp my head off.

"Aaahhhh!" I drop my phone and cover my head with both arms. Then I remember the soft kiss on my cheek, and my heart rate slows down a little. I lift my head to risk another look at the beast. My phone light shines at the monster. It looks like a cross between a wolf and a tiger with stripes across its back and tail. You don't want to meet either in a dark place . . . yet it seems friendly. I slowly reach out my hand, fingers curled under to let it smell me. My Grandpa taught me to do this with dogs. He loved all creatures, and he wasn't afraid of anything. Now that I've been reading his journals, I feel he's always with me.

The creature comes closer and puts its soft snout in my hand like a handshake. I have to smile as the bristly whiskers tickle my fingers.

"So, where are we, Wolfie?" I ask, not expecting an answer. I pick up my phone and shine the light around to see we're in an underground cave. There's no air movement at all. But it's beautiful—rock walls and ledges of spiky crystals sparkle pink and grey back at me. Eerie passageways create a labyrinth with tunnels leading deep into a cavern. I can hear running water in the distance and dripping all around me. What a stink! Pew, like a sewer!

Long tubes hang from the ceiling like icicles and sprout up from the cave floor, making columns when they meet. My grandpa told me these are called stalactites and stalagmites. When he took me spelunking in Mammoth Cave one summer, he taught me how to remember which is which—the 'C' in stalactite is for ceiling, and the 'G' in stalagmite is for ground. These are so big they probably took a gazillion years to form, one drip at a time.

"Let's go find my friends," I tell Wolfie, crawling around holes full of water. Wolfie's long, pointy ears point to the left, and he whines loudly, startling me. "What is it, boy?" I ask. "Are my friends that way?" He whines again, and I can almost pick up his thoughts with my ESP. *Negative.*

I hear noises in the other direction. I hope it's Matt and Celeste coming towards my cell phone light. "Over here, guys!" I call out as I head toward them.

"Hawk!" I hear from the tunnel, and the creature runs off in the direction his ears were pointing.

"Wolfie, wait up!" I call out, worried that I'll be abandoned by the only living being I know on the planet.

CHAPTER 7

CAVE OF WONDERS

"Hawk, come here with your flashlight! Celeste is hurt," Matt calls from the darkness.

I crawl towards the sound of his voice with my cell phone out in front of me. The cave is high enough for me to stand up and walk, but it's safer to crawl because of the jagged rocks and holes everywhere. "Hey, guys. Where are you?" I gasp. The air is muggy down here.

"Over here. Hurry Hawk. We need your light." I hear Matt who's pretty close now.

I see Celeste sitting down, leaning against the cave wall, as Matt beckons me over. "It's good that you have your phone with you, buddy. Shine it over here so we can see Celeste's ankle."

"Yup, I rolled my ankle in one of those small craters. I feel so stupid," she says, rubbing her ankle, which looks like it's starting to swell up a little. "I don't know if I can walk."

My grandpa taught me how to survive in the woods when he took me camping. One time I fell down a hill and sprained my wrist, so he wrapped it with his bandana and brought me to the stream for cold water. I now know why he taught me these survival skills. He was preparing me for cosmic adventures like this.

"My grandpa told me when you have a sprain, you need PIE," I say.

"My ankle is sore. Why would I want pie?" cries Celeste, sniffing.

"It stands for pressure, ice, and elevation—the three best things to do when you sprain your ankle," I explain. "Here, take off your shoe and put your foot in this hole full of cold water," I instruct her as I hunt around for something to wrap it with. "Matt, are you wearing a belt? We could wrap it around her ankle for support."

"Okay, but how am I going to keep my pants up?" he asks, taking off his belt and handing it to me.

"Don't worry. We've seen your underwear before!" I joke, smiling at him, "Ha-ha, very funny! You're lucky I put a clean pair on this morning," he says, snorting as we high-five.

"Enough with the jokes, you guys. Have you forgotten that we're underground on a remote planet, a million light-years from home? And we're supposed to be looking for Big Mikey," Celeste reminds us.

"Sorry, Celeste. Let's see if you can crawl a bit," I say sheepishly.

Celeste starts to crawl and then screams as a huge, hairy beast with big teeth comes bounding out of the darkness and leaps up on my chest, almost knocking me over.

"Wolfie!"

CHAPTER 8

CRY WOLF

Wolfie and I have a happy reunion as Matt and Celeste freeze and watch with wide eyes.

"W-what is that thing, Hawk?" Matt asks, his voice shaking.

"Not what, who. This is Wolfie, a very smart dog I met earlier." Wolfie sits down and wags his tail. I always wanted a dog like this. A nice, furry . . . great dane . . . mixed with a—a snow leopard. I smile as I imagine my mom's face if I brought Wolfie home. "I hope he can lead us out of here. So be nice. Here, offer him your hand to sniff," I tell them.

They both reach out their hands, and Wolfie sniffs, then licks them, making Celeste giggle. Matt's eyes are squeezed shut in fear. But they pop open as Wolfie nuzzles and licks his hand.

"Ooooh, dog slobber. Yuck!" Matt cries, but I notice he's now petting Wolfie's thick, stripy fur.

"Okay, Wolfie, show us how to get out of here," I say, as I reach out a hand to Celeste and help her up. "Let's do our arm-in-arm thing to help Celeste walk, Matt," I suggest, handing him the flashlight. We know Celeste is sensitive about her personal space or touching too much because of her Asperger's Syndrome, so we link arms with her instead of wrapping our arms around her for support. She'll tolerate it, especially when she's in a dark place . . . and she's sprained her ankle.

Wolfie looks at us and whines, pointing his ears again towards a tunnel that goes deeper into the cave. "What is it, boy?" I ask him, and he looks at us with hopeful eyes. Then he dashes off towards the tunnel.

"What should we do, Hawk? I think he wants us to follow him." Matt says shining the light towards the tunnel as his striped tail disappears around a curve.

"Let's follow him for a bit, but then we have to get out of here and find Big Mikey. Agreed?" I ask making sure I have Celeste in a strong elbow hold.

"Agreed," they both say together.

"Wolfie, wait up!" I call as we hobble down the tunnel after him. Matt holds the phone up, pointing ahead of us to see where to step, but we are much slower than our four-legged guide. The cool cave feels downright cold as we shiver and slide deeper into the darkness. It smells moldy, like old sweaty socks, and it's hard to breathe. Up ahead, I see the tip of Wolfie's tail disappear around a corner, and it spurs us on.

"How are you holding up, Celeste?" Matt asks, as we avoid a large crack on the cave floor.

"Much better now. I think the belt is helping. I hope your pants are holding up." She jokes, leaning on our arms. We are chuckling when we hear a distant howl of pain.

"Wolfie!" I call out as Matt, Celeste, and I look around, trembling.

"What was that?!" Matt hisses, shining the phone light all around.

"I don't know, but I think Wolfie's in trouble," I grunt, as we help Celeste sit down and take a break.

"Thanks, Hawk. I think I can walk by myself now," Celeste says, rubbing her ankle.

"Let's go down a little further to see if he needs help," I say to them.

"Okay, but slowly," Celeste says as we help her up.

We make our way down the winding passages. The cave walls glisten as water comes down like sheets of a waterfall and pools in the craters. My grandpa would call this a 'living cave' because of all the water—it's still growing. Large crystal formations loom ahead of us like giant marble columns as the tunnel opens up into a huge chamber with a 100-foot high ceiling. It dazzles us, like a church cathedral.

"Whoa, you could fit a skyscraper in here!" Matt says, whistling. We hear a repeat of the whistle as it echoes off the chamber walls.

"This is lit!" I say, cupping my ear to hear anything else echoing in the cave. We hear someone or something approaching from a distance, and we scramble to hide behind a wide column. Tripping and panting, my heart pounds in my chest. Two strange figures in hooded robes, holding sticks and lanterns, approach with Wolfie between them.

"We told you to stay out of our way. Now you will suffer the consequences." They roughly throw him down and taser him with their sticks. Wolfie howls in pain and then just lays there unmoving.

We all look at each other in alarm but wait for the aliens to disappear back down the passage. Once they

are out of sight, we rush over to where Wolfie is lying down, unconscious. He isn't breathing, so we roll him over onto his back and feel for a heartbeat on either side of his chest.

"Let's try CPR, like they showed us in health class," I say, moving around Wolfie.

"On a dog! Will that work?" Matt asks, looking from me to Celeste.

"It's worth a try," says Celeste, pushing on Wolfie's chest.

"I think we have to blow air into his nose first." We look at one another, waiting for a volunteer. "Okay, Matt, you and Celeste press on either side of his chest, and I'll blow some air into his nose," I instruct. They press down, and we hear air moving out. I take Wolfie's snout in both of my hands and gently blow air into his nose. We repeat this until we see he's breathing on his own, and his tongue lolls out to lick his lips. We smile and do high-fives as Wolfie opens his eyes and looks at us. His stripy tail lifts once and falls back down — he's exhausted.

"Poor Wolfie. They almost killed you! Why did they do that?" I ask him, stroking his soft thick fur. I look into his eyes, and I get a thought from him. "*Kyp* . . . *Kyp* . . . *Kyp* . . . *Kyp*." It's more of a sound than a word.

"What does *Kyp* mean?" I ask Matt and Celeste as I try to make the unusual sound. "Wolfie keeps thinking about *Kyp*."

"Maybe *Kyp* is why they tasered him," Matt says, petting him.

"Maybe *Kyp* is his person . . . err alien," Celeste says

as Wolfie looks at her and whines. "That's it! He's trying to get to his alien-person," she continues, as Wolfie's stripy tail thumps the ground next to us.

"Help me hide Wolfie behind this column so he can rest. Then we'll see if we can find his owner," I try to sound confident. But if they did this to Wolfie . . . what would they do to us?!

CHAPTER 9

LABYRINTHS OF LABYRINTHIA

We creep down the passageway the two aliens took. We are stealthy so as not to alert anyone to our presence. So far, we have the advantage—the element of surprise. As we descend, it gets darker, colder, and deathly silent. Celeste suddenly stops. "I can't go any further. I'm claustrophobic."

"Closet-what?" whispers Matt.

"Not closet, claustro-phobic, like the walls are closing in on us," she tells Matt.

"Oh, I thought that was a fear of Santa Claus. Get it? 'Claus'-trophobic!" Matt jokes to lighten the mood when we hear a loud BANG further down the tunnel. We all stop with our mouths open, Matt's arm hanging, mid high-five.

"What was that?" I whisper, looking at Matt and Celeste.

BANG! TAP! BANG!

"It's coming from over here!" I say, half-running, half-dragging Celeste and Matt with me towards a tunnel to our right.

We get down on all fours and crawl through a small shaft toward some light and the banging sounds. We keep crawling until we come to a rock wall, and we can tell the noise is coming from the other side.

"Matt, stand up and peek over the wall!" I whisper-hiss.

"No, you do it. It's your turn," he argues.

Right on cue, Celeste stands up and looks over the wall. Her hands fly to her mouth to stop herself from screaming as she falls back to the ground.

"What is it, Celeste?" I say.

"Is it a dragon? Is it Smaug?" Matt asks, and I can tell he's hoping it is. I shake my head and shoot him a 'Don't say that!' look. Celeste takes her hands from her mouth, but she still can't talk. She points at the top of the wall to suggest we should look for ourselves. Matt and I look at each other and slowly stand up, looking over the wall. At first, we don't understand what we are seeing. There are dozens of small beings in a pit, working with hammers, tapping on the walls. Their faces, lit up by lanterns, are black with soot and they have chains like metal leashes around their legs. But we can tell that these are children. What the heck . . . this is like dragon's breath—it stinks!

"This is some kind of prison for kids," Matt whispers. "This is bad, Hawk. It's terribad—terrible and bad put together."

"Maybe Wolfie was trying to rescue his owner, and that's why they tasered him," I tell the others as we drop back down.

"What can we do?" Celeste says, wiping her eyes and nose on her sleeve. Then her eyes go wide. "What if Big Mikey's down there?"

All three of us poke our heads over the wall for another look. The captives are mostly hairless, so they

look like babies, with pointy ears and yellow eyes that are big and far apart. Their skin, under all the dirt, is a greenish color making them look sick. Big Mikey would definitely stand out in this crowd, and I'm thankful that I don't see him. They are digging something out of the walls with their little hammers. Some have dug tunnels into the wall and are filling buckets with the rubble. If someone slows down, a boss goes over and shakes him. The bosses look like bigger, meaner, and hairier versions of their prisoners.

"I think Yoda's from around here," Matt says, noticing the resemblance.

"Yeah, they look . . . humanoid," I whisper back.

"These little aliens should be in school or, or whatever they have to teach kids on this planet," states Celeste angrily. Then we hear a sound that stops us cold. *"Kyp!"*

CHAPTER 10

DIGGING FOR GOLD?

All the bosses run over to where a child was work-ing, but now, only a broken chain remains. They hold up the empty leash, point at the tunnels, and then they all run off in different directions. Matt, Celeste, and I sit down to figure this out.

"Do you think Wolfie's alien-person escaped?" I ask the others.

"Yes. I think he knew Wolfie was trying to get to him, so he broke free," whispers Celeste.

"Maybe he saw them dragging Wolfie out and heard him crying," Matt adds quietly.

"Let's try to backtrack and find him. Maybe we can help him and let him know about Wolfie," I say.

"We're supposed to be looking for Big Mikey, remember," says Celeste grimly.

"Maybe we'll find them both hiding somewhere in this cave," I suggest, trying to be positive.

"Hawk, we can't leave all these kids down here. This is slavery. My Paw told me that slavery is not cool. No matter where it's happening. We have to help them, too," whispers Matt.

"You're right, Matt. But let's find Kyp first, so we can get some more information about what's going on here," I tell him.

"Okay, let's do this!" I say, as we do our secret

clubhouse handshake. We link fingers, do an interlocking fist pump, and then click our rings together.
We crawl out of the shaft without our flashlight, so
they don't spot us. It's slow going, not to mention the
puddles. I keep hearing splashes and Celeste mut-
tering under her breath, "I got another soaker!" We
keep going until we are all totally wet to the skin and
shivering.

"H-h-hawk, I'm f-f-f-freezing. I know how those
p-p-poor kids feel down here all the t-t-time," says
Matt with his teeth chattering.

"Me too!" Celeste gasps behind me. "L-l-let's f-find
some place to warm up a bit."

I briefly turn on my phone light and see a small
opening in the wall up ahead. "This way," I urge.
"There's a small cave up ahead where we can rest."

We clamber into the cave and flop on the ground,
exhausted.

"Turn on your flashlight, Hawk. I'll block the opening with my backpack," says Matt.

"G-good idea, M-M-Matt," I say, my teeth chattering as I fumble with my phone. Lighting up the small
cave, I see Celeste's dirty, tear-streaked face, and
behind her, a stranger is lurking in the shadows.

"Aaahhh!" I drop my phone in surprise and do
a backward crab walk. "Who's there?" I shout, and
Celeste scrambles behind me as I pick up my phone.
Shining the light into the back of the cave, we see a
miserable-looking creature. Dirty from head to toe,
almost naked, he's shaking from the cold. We see it's
one of the alien slaves, and he's scared—probably of us!

I am the closest to him, and I see that his little, yellowish-green face is all scrunched up and wrinkled. I can't tell if he's old or young. His long forehead ends with a bit of dark hair that starts in the middle of his head, and his big yellow eyes are far apart. I try ESP.

Hello. Don't be afraid. We are from planet Earth. We want to help you . . . and Wolfie. As soon as I say it, I think about the big leopard-wolf with the soft fur and stripy tail. The boy alien looks over, and for the first time, his eyes light up.

"You know my Eiflow?" he mumbles in a language we don't understand, but I can tell what he's saying with ESP. I translate his words.

We all look at him and nod, then look at each other and smile. We found Kyp.

"Kyp?" I ESP, noticing his surprise that I know his name.

CHAPTER 11

WHAT A MAZE!

"Here, take my gym shirt," Matt says, pulling a wrinkled shirt out of his backpack and handing it to Kyp.

When he pulls it over his head, it goes down to the ground like a dress with our team name and Matt's number on the front; Panthers 66. Although it's a little stinky, Kyp looks a lot warmer in the shirt.

I whisper to them, "Okay, so here's the plan. We go back to where Wolfie is hiding to get him. We set all the child slaves free and stop these evil bosses from ever doing this again."

"Then we'll find Big Mikey," Celeste adds, looking at me sideways.

"Uhhh," I stammer, as I almost forgot about him. "Yup, then we'll find Big Mikey. It's all part of the plan." *I just don't know what the plan is yet!*

We know we have to do something after Kyp tells us that the slave drivers go down into the small villages and walk through the streets playing some sleepy music that makes the young ones stop what they are doing and follow them. The younglings go into a trance and follow the music down into the mines of Labyrinthia. They are charmed and hypnotized by the magical music and then led deep into the cave. The bosses force them to work in the maze for nothing more than bread and water. Once they're in the mine maze, there's no way out.

"Wait!" blurts Celeste. "This sounds like the creepy Pied Piper and his magical flute. This piper guy would play his flute, and all the rats followed him out of town, but when they didn't pay him he ended up luring all the children out of town, too."

"Whoa, what did they have to do? Break his flute or play it backwards to get the children to come back?" laughs Matt.

"No, the legend says that he lured them into the river where they drowned . . . like the rats. That story gave me nightmares when I was little." Celeste shivers, as we all think about what she just said.

Kyp adds, "The village elders warn not to follow the 'ombres' or the sleep-walking children because if the trance is broken, the village will be forever cursed." Kyp looks down. "But they are sad now that the children are gone. I have been here for seven tri-suns . . . Eiflow was looking for me. He's not afraid to be cursed."

"But what are they digging for down here?" I ask him.

"Powerful prisms that absorb the tri-sun energy and refract it. Put many together and you have enough energy to blow a planet to bits." He looks down, adding, "The prisms are called Shoq-lot."

Matt, Celeste, and I look at each other with our mouths hanging open, "Did he say Chocolate?" Matt says.

Kyp darts for the opening in the wall, "Must find Eiflow. He is cursed, and it is my fault!"

PANTHERS
66

"Hey, wait for us," I say, shaking my head, trying to understand how that sweet, delicious treat we all love could be so powerful and dangerous. We crawl out of the cave after Kyp. I ESP Kyp an image of the large church chamber with the high ceilings and columns where we left Wolfie.

"I know that place. This way," says Kyp, starting to run, used to this dark underground terrain. His short legs and wide feet navigate the craters and cracks with no problem. Crawling along, Matt, Celeste, and I can hardly keep up with him. We have no choice. We stand up, link arms for support, and run after the disappearing alien boy in the Panthers dress.

"I think he went this way," I whisper, shining my phone down a long tunnel, imagining I saw a blue satin jersey disappearing around the bend.

"Kyp!" Matt and I ESP him, hoping he'll slow down and show us the way.

We head for the open area up ahead. "Okay, this looks familiar." I shine my light around the large cavern, with shiny stalagmites and stalactites decorating the grotto. "There he is!" I point to the other side, where Kyp is bending down behind an icy column. "Come on!" We run over and see Kyp hugging Wolfie. Wolfie licks his face weakly and tries to stand up. His tail is wagging, but he falls back down again.

"Wolfie!" I say, bending down to grab his soft furry face, "Come on, boy, we have to get out of here!" I ESP him the images. He looks from Kyp to me and back again, his tail thumping on the cold floor. He tries once more to stand, and it works. On wobbly legs, he goes to Kyp and puts his snout in his hand, and closes his eyes with a small sigh. Kyp hugs him, then leans over to say something in Wolfie's ear.

Wolfie turns to me and limps over to lick my hand. Then he does the same to both Matt and Celeste. He looks at us, sits down, and makes a deep sound like a growling purr. "Eiflow says thank you for saving his life," Kyp looks at us with tears in his bright yellow eyes. "Will you help my friends too? Like me, they are sick and need to see our fire star, Tri-sun, to be well."

"We can try," I whisper, looking at Matt and Celeste for their approval. Matt steps toward me with his hand up, and Celeste does the same. We link fingers, do an interlocking fist pump, and click our rings together. "Let's do it!"

CHAPTER 12

LOST IN LABYRINTHIA

Kyp and Wolfie lead the way back down through the tunnels, sliding deeper and deeper into the mine. The going is slow, and we are cold to the bone, except for Wolfie, who has the perfect fur coat for these caves. Wolfie prances along and looks happily over at Kyp, who is almost at eye level with him. He keeps a reassuring hand on Wolfie's warm head or his soft furry back. I can tell they were apart for a long time and missed each other. I really hope we can help them escape this underground jail and go back to their families. But how? There's a murmuring up ahead that jolts me out of my thoughts . . . and it's getting closer.

We all look around, but there's nowhere to go. We can't stay here, and it's too late to hide. The columns are too far away, and the goons are too close. *What do we do?!* They're about to come around the corner and see us right there in the open when something crazy happens—we float up like we're filling up with helium. I flounder around to get my balance as we grab hands and rise toward the ceiling of the cavern. I look down and see the goons pass under us; their lanterns light up the area. The tops of their heads shine, and long ears stick out at the sides like ears of corn. Celeste smiles at me and focuses her power to levitate us gently and as quietly as possible. Kyp and Wolfie cling desperately to each other—confused and terrified. I ESP them, "It'll be okay. It's Celeste's super-power."

I feel something bump the top of my head. "Youch!" I look around at all the pointy tips of the stalactites hanging down from the ceiling like icicles. I look over at Matt, who has an icicle spearing his afro and looks like he's going to puke. Kyp grabs onto the giant icicle next to him as Celeste pulls the trembling Wolfie in close to her body. She keeps him from floating up into the stalactites. From the cave ceiling, I look down at the last of the goons and notice some keys on a ring dangling from a hook on his belt. I ESP to Celeste to levitate the keys, and she easily lifts the ring off the belt and floats it up to me. When the coast is clear, we sink back down to the ground like our balloons are deflating. "That was awesome, Celeste!" Matt and I high-five. Kyp looks at her with big, round, yellow eyes. He thinks Earthlings are magical creatures right now!

Celeste looks away. "I didn't even think about what to do. I just reacted to the danger. I was as surprised as you guys!" she says—cool about saving our butts again.

"Yeah, and I didn't even puke this time!" Matt says, proud that he didn't *blow* our cover.

We go silent as we follow Kyp. Our bodies press up against the cold, rough walls to stay out of sight. Suddenly, a bone-shattering screech forces us to put our hands over our ears. Poor Wolfie drops to the ground and covers his head with his paws. The horrid sound builds to an ear-piercing shriek, then recedes like a passing train. My stomach tightens, and the hair on the back of my neck stands on end.

"What the heck is that?" I wail, ESPing Kyp, while I shine my phone light on the cave walls.

"That is the Silver Hellion," says Kyp, petting Wolfie. "It arrives at 90 degrees of the Tri-Sun every microt."

"It s-s-sounds angry!" says Celeste, crying now and still covering her sensitive ears, though the screech is distant.

"What's a Silver Hellion?" Matt asks the question we are all wondering.

"It is the monster we must feed so that it does not eat us. It is always angry . . . and hungry," Kyp says matter-of-factly. "His wide mouth has spiky teeth and breathes fire. He has a long neck and a long tail. You cannot hide from his cold eyes."

"What?!" Celeste and I look at each other, stunned.

"S-sounds like a dragon. I-I'm glad it didn't stop h-h-here!" Matt shivers from cold, fear, or both.

"We must go there now. Everyone will be unchained, and the bosses will be busy feeding the Hellion, so we can slip past them." Kyp takes off with Wolfie towards the screaming banshee.

Matt lags behind us, "I don't want to meet up with the hangry alien dragon that's waiting for his dinner." He searches the darkness for any sign of the shark-toothed Silver Hellion.

"Don't worry, Matt, here, you can borrow my extra stone," Celeste says, handing him a cool, smooth, worry stone she keeps in her pocket.

"Thanks, Celeste," Matt says, pocketing the stone and rubbing it. "I feel better already. Maybe we can get some chocolate crystals, too."

"C'mon, let's catch up to Kyp and Wolfie," I say, tugging them by our linked arms. We follow Wolfie's tail like a waving flag.

CHAPTER 13

CAN YOU DIG IT?

I don't know how, but Kyp leads us back to the rock wall at the edge of the work pit. We stash ourselves in a small nook where we can watch everything going on below without being seen. We poke our heads over the wall and see the raggedly dressed little aliens. They struggle with their loaded buckets as they get in line and go out of sight with whatever they dug out of the pit. There are no bosses around, so we assume they are feeding the Hellion buckets full of . . . what? Rocks? Crystals? I try to remember what Mr. Brainer told us about mines in the geology lesson. He said miners dig for metals, gold, silver, and even diamonds underground. What does this alien mine-monster eat? Chocolate meteorites?

The eerie screaming starts up again, and a small alien flies into view. The poor little guy stumbles and rolls over and over, finally coming to a stop. A bucket comes flying out after him, landing a few feet away. I don't think the Hellion liked what he fed him. We watch as he crawls on his hands and knees towards the wall dragging his bucket with him. He looks terrified as he hammers on the wall, looking around for some unseen danger. A boss comes out of a tunnel and marches angrily over to him, and tasers him on the neck. The boy flops onto his side and lies still. We look

at each other with wide eyes, our mouths hanging open. We're not sure what to do.

I ESP Kyp, "That's what they did to Wolfie." We look at each other and reach down to pet the soft, furry snout between us.

"That is my friend, Babu. He never digs enough ore to satisfy Silver Hellion," Kyp tells us. "Babu will be okay. The bosses only stun us with their tasers." Sure enough, Babu struggles to sit up and starts hammering at the wall again.

"Kids shouldn't have to work like this, especially under the ground where there's no fresh air or sunshine. This is child labor and kidnapping or alien-napping or something illegal. These kids should be with their parents," whispers Celeste, getting angry. We look around for a way to help them.

"Too bad we don't have those giant roaches like on Bilaluna," Matt exclaims, pounding his fist into his palm. "We could pile everyone inside and bulldoze our way out of this pit." He looks around, hopeful for a cyborg roach-coach.

"Hold on, Matt, that's brilliant!" says Celeste.

"Wait, I'm brilliant?" says Matt, confused.

"Yes, you are. If we can get everyone into a giant bulldozer, we can break out of here!" exclaims Celeste.

"Woohoo! I'm so brilliant, I . . . wait a sec . . . we don't have a bulldozer!" he says, scratching his head.

"Maybe we do?" says Celeste, looking towards where we last heard the Silver Hellion. Right on cue, the Hellion starts to scream again, and we all close our eyes and cover our ears. The horrible, ear-shattering sound is echoing through the cave and off the walls.

"Oh no! No, no, no, no Celeste." Matt pleads when the sound quiets down, and another little alien comes tumbling into view with his bucket. "I'm not going anywhere near that... that *hangry* monster! I saw the episode of 'Star Trekkers', where they had to defeat the two-jawed Giax from Gorgon. I'll never unsee those snapping jaws. It ate everything in its path!"

"It'll be okay, Matt. Celeste can control it with her telekinesis." I look over at Celeste, who's nodding.

The Hellion screams again like it's saying—*Just try it! Make my day.*

Matt collapses next to Wolfie and covers his head.

"Besides, the Hellion is the only thing that knows the way out of this maze," I whisper.

CHAPTER 14

WHO'S THE BOSS?

We huddle together around Wolfie to discuss our plan . . . and for the warmth of his long, soft fur.

"Okay, here's what we're going to do," I whisper, "Matt, you and I will throw rocks in different directions to cause a distraction. When the bosses run off to find out what's happening, Celeste, Kyp, and Wolfie will go down into the pit and round up the alien kids." I look towards the small alien. "Kyp will tell them that we are friendly and want to help them escape." I give a little smile. "Celeste, see if you can control the Hellion and transport us all out of this death pit." Celeste grins back and nods, as I continue, "Matt and I will join you down there as soon as we know the goons are out of earshot. Remember, everyone, we have to work fast. Let's do this!"

We high-five, then Matt and I look around for rocks to throw into the passageways. Celeste and her team get ready to go down into the pit as soon as the coast is clear. I point at Matt, and throw rocks away from the pit. Thunk! Thud! Bonk! The sound of large rocks hitting and skittering across the cave floor echo all over the pit. A hush falls over the mine as the aliens and bosses look around, not sure what is happening. We see the bosses talking together then rush off down different passageways, and I point at Celeste and Kyp to go.

"Now!" I hiss.

Matt and I pause our rock tossing to watch Celeste and Kyp make their way down into the pit, with Wolfie following. It's like watching a silent movie play out. When the little aliens see them approach, they back away, terrified of Wolfie and Celeste. They hang back while Kyp frantically explains what is happening. Waving his arms, jumping up and down, and pointing, he convinces them to follow him towards the Silver Hellion. A small army of dirty, exhausted alien creatures march out of sight. Our plan is working.

Matt and I throw the last of our rocks and get ready to hurry down to the pit when something grabs us by the shoulders.

"Aaaaahh!" I jump and turn my head, my heart thundering in my chest. The other part of our plan fails because we are in the clutches of an alien boss with a death grip on us. I stare in shock at the yellowish-green face and white mohawk of the alien with such bad breath that Matt and I start to gag and choke. My hands fly up to cover my nose. Blech! Dead fish, rotten eggs, and dog poop all rolled into one nasty weapon of halitosis.

"Aaaaahh! Let's get out of here, Matt! I'm going to puke!" I yell through my fingers. But the boss-grip is so strong that we can't even get away from his breath. Matt tries to kick him in the shin, but it's useless. We fall to the ground, and we're dragged by the scruffs of our necks, out of our hiding spot and away from freedom.

"Noooooo!" I shriek, kicking my feet out in defiance. I don't want to be a child slave.

"Let us go, ya big goon!" Matt yells at the alien, who ignores our feeble fight and hauls us over the rough cave floor. We kick and splash through puddles when we hear the Silver Hellion screeching from deep in the mine. The goon pauses and then quickens his pace. I wonder if Celeste and Kyp are taking control of the 'Jaws' monster at this very moment. I'm excited for about one second—then I realize Matt and I will be left behind in this child prison camp.

I ESP Matt frantically, *Matt, we've got to get away!*

Yeah, I know. He ESPs back, gasping for air.

I slide my eyeballs to the right to see Matt wrestling with his collar as he starts to turn blue. That didn't even happen to him on planet Ka'Azula!

Matt, breathe! I ESP him just as the boss releases our collars and drops us onto the cold stone floor like two bags of dirty laundry. We are gasping and choking as we hear him fumbling with his keys. Jangle, Jangle Click. Then he throws us into a dank, stinky cave and leaves us there. At least we can breathe again! OMG, it smells like rotting vegetables in here . . . or something dead. *Pew!* I gulp as much of the disgusting air as I can into my lungs, choking and crawling on my hands and knees. Matt is wheezing and trying to sit up, but I think he's okay, too. I pull out my phone and turn on the flashlight app, and it lights up the small grotto. I look around at the rock walls and the far corners to see if there's some way to escape.

"Aaaaahh!" I jump towards Matt when I see bones in the corner, and I'm not sure if they're animal, alien or . . .

"What are we going to do if they never come back for us?" Matt says, eyeing the pile of bones in the corner. His eyes go big as he thinks of something else and grabs my arm. "Celeste and Kyp won't leave without us? Will they?"

"I don't know! C'mon, let's try the door." Matt and I crawl over to the door, and we're just about to push on it when we hear the goons run by on the other side. We leap back, away from the door, and cling to each other in the dark. We're afraid, but I think they are too! We've caused some chaos in their dark workhouse, and they're not sure what's going on.

CHAPTER 15

DO YOU KNOW THE WAY TO HAMELIN?

"Push, Matt!" I hiss through clenched teeth. We try to break through the heavy door before the goons come back, but it won't budge.

"Owww!" says Matt, rubbing his leg, "Something scratched me." He pushes against the door with all his might.

"Ouch! What is that?" he says, moving away from me. "Hawk, what's in your pocket?"

"Not now, Matt. I'm busy!" I'm forcing my whole body against the rock-solid door when Matt reaches into my jeans pocket and pulls out the long dangling key on its ring. I open my eyes and look at the key, and it hits me . . .

"We have the key! We–Have–The–Key!" I dance and grab the keys from Matt. *Thank you, Celeste!* I ESP.

Jangle, Clang, Click. The heavy door swings inward, and we peek out, looking both ways before we make a break for it. We have to get back to Celeste, Kyp, and Wolfie before they escape without us. *We're coming, guys! Wait for us!* I ESP them.

Matt and I sprint out of the cave, and I fall over a big stalagmite in our path.

"Aaargh! Help me up, Matt!"

The icicles are cold and sharp. We walk as fast as we can in the dark, navigating the obstacle course of craters and icicles blocking our way. We need to retrace our steps and get back to the pit. I hear something below us, and I put my arm out to stop Matt. I put my finger to my lips and point downwards because there's a goon with a lantern one level down. We press ourselves against the dripping cave wall, and I take a slurp of the icy cold water as it runs down my face. Brrrr! I shiver and try to blend into the rock as we inch along. My vision starts to blur, and I get dizzy.

What's happening? I look back at Matt. I've been in this cave too long. Moving around underground with no visible landmarks is making me feel weird. My head is spinning, and I have trouble telling up from down. My sense of balance is all messed up. I put my arms out to steady myself so I don't fall off the edge. Panic rises in me because we're lost, and I imagine we'll be left down here forever. I sit down and put my head in my hands. I can't move. We could get lost and never get home. Matt sits down next to me. I have to tell him that I can't go on when I hear a voice—*Come on, Hawk. You can do this!*

"Who said that?" I whisper, looking at Matt.

"Huh? What is it?" He whispers back, looking around.

Remember what I taught you about caves? You must listen with your whole body if you want to get out of here.

"I can't do it!" I moan. I must be hallucinating.

Follow the sound of my voice, Hawk . . . come on lad . . . get yourself moving.

When he calls me lad, I know it's my grandpa. But his voice is getting distant, so I get up and tug Matt by the arm.

Who Said that?

"Wait!" I sob, stumbling and staggering toward his comforting voice. I lurch blindly forward, where he tells me to go.

That's it, lad. You're almost there.

Suddenly, the screech of the Hellion blocks out all other sounds. It's very close now, and almost a welcome sound because it's our way out.

"This way." I pull Matt to the left, towards the wailing banshee, and see the rock wall above the pit up ahead. "We made it!" I send out a silent prayer. *Thank you, Grandpa.*

I try to high-five Matt, but I'm so shaky I miss his hand. We crouch in front of the wall and peek over the top into the pit. There's no one around, but I can't shake the eerie feeling that a goon will grab my shoulder any second.

"Let's go find Celeste." We stumble our way down the steep spiral slope into the pit, careful not to slip or make gravel spill out in front of us. It's exhausting because we're dehydrated and almost out of energy.

We hear footsteps in the distance, and fear tightens my stomach as we duck down behind a boulder. But the goons don't enter the pit, and the footsteps keep going right past us. Matt and I look at each other and nod. *Whew! That was close.* Heartbeats hammering in our ears, we reach the bottom of the pit. I scan the area looking for some sign of Celeste, Kyp, Wolfie . . . or a hangry Hellion.

CHAPTER 16

WELCOME TO MY NIGHTMARE

It's bright in the pit, with lanterns on every wall. We get a better look at this giant arena from inside. It's twenty to thirty feet high and one hundred feet wide, with rock pillars holding it up. Long tubes hang down from the ceiling and look like weird alien worms. I remember I found it funny when my grandpa told me these are called 'soda straws.' Looking at them reminds me that I'd love a cola and milk right now. I lick my dry lips just thinking about it and gaze around at the wonders of the cavern.

"It looks like a medieval castle down here," I whisper to Matt, who's getting ahead of me. Multicolored rock formations loom in the background, and crystals of cave popcorn cover the walls. The giant rock formations spark my imagination, and I see a bear standing on his hind legs reaching for me, and there's one that looks like my grandpa's armchair.

Lower down, the walls are full of holes where the workers were hammering at threads of jewels in the rock. All this pain, just for some silly crystals.

I stumble over a heavy chain left behind where the slaves fled. The floor and walls beyond the large chamber branch out like a tree. Winding paths lead to passageways and smaller caves. Down one of the larger paths there is a round, bluish-green pool in a cavern that looks like the view of planet Earth from space. I swallow hard and fight back the tears when I think about home. I wipe my nose and look up at the ceiling. Above the pool there's a giant chandelier made of stalactites, and it reflects the light with glittery cave ribbons and cave pearls that dance on the upper walls of the cavern.

"Wow!" I'm about to point it out to Matt when I see two big yellow eyes in a green face staring down at me from the top level.

"L-let's get out of here!" I stammer, catching up to Matt in the passage leading to the Hellion.

We creep down the well-worn tunnel easily. No stalagmites here, but neither are Celeste and Kyp.

"How far would they go without us?" Matt asks, running his fingers through his dusty afro.

"I don't know, Matt," I am worried too. I haven't had an ESP message from any of them in a long time. "The Hellion was in this tunnel before, so let's keep going."

Matt must have read my mind because he punches his fist into his palm and says, "This is like that episode of 'Star Trekkers' where the good guys make hats out of aluminum foil to block the aliens from reading their thoughts."

Oh, brother! "Why would they wear tin foil hats?" I hiss as we hurry along the corridor.

"To block their brain waves, of course! So the aliens won't figure out their plans," he exclaims.

I get a vision of Celeste and Kyp chained up with pointy aluminum foil hats on their heads. I shake my head, "That didn't work, remember? Tinfoil only made the reception better." I remind him when something with big fangs comes out of the shadows.

"Aaaaahh!" We yelp in surprise.

"Wait, it's Wolfie!" I cry as I help Matt off the cave floor where Wolfie is standing over him, licking his face.

"Good boy, Wolfie!" I grab his large, furry head in a big hug and feel him sigh as if releasing a big stress. I've never been so happy to see a large, hairy alien before. "You found us! C'mon, let's get out of here!" I stand up and start walking, but Wolfie lays down and puts his paws over his snout.

"What is it, boy?" asks Matt, bending over to pet him. But Wolfie looks at us and whimpers like a sad dog. Suddenly I get pictures in my mind showing Celeste and Kyp being tossed into a tiny closet some-where. Wolfie is psychic!

"Take us to Kyp, Wolfie!" I say, and he perks up and trots up the passageway with us right behind him.

"Where could they be, Hawk?" Matt asks, leaping over a wide opening in the ground in front of us.

"We'll find out, and then we're getting out of this alien underworld," I say, leaping over the crevasse without thinking. It's only a foot and a half wide. What could go wrong?

"Aaaahh!" I misjudge the distance in the dark, and my front foot hits the inside edge of the hole. I'm going down the crevasse, clawing at the edge of the cave floor and kicking my feet, trying to find a hold on the wall.

"Matt, help me!" I slide further down, taking dirt and rocks with me. I hear them bouncing from side to side before landing with a dull thud at the bottom a long way down. I don't want to experience that ride, so I use the last of my strength and my fingernails to

hang on until Matt runs back and grabs my arm. He hauls back with all his might. Wolfie is behind Matt, yanking his hoodie with his teeth. I pull and kick and finally get my footing on a protruding rock. Matt helps me climb up and over the edge, gasping and panting.

"Thanks, bud! I owe you one," I cough, rolling over onto my back.

"You can pay me in moon pies!" He says, huffing and puffing. "I'm so hungry right now I could eat a hundred of them. Ummmm!"

"Okay, I'll get you a whole box." I lay there thinking. "Hey, I just got an idea. Let's cover up the hole so that when the goons come after us, and they WILL come after us, they'll fall into it."

"Great idea, Hawk. Here, use my black hoodie. It's all we've got," Matt says, taking off his hooded sweater and shivering in his T-shirt.

"You'll freeze, dude," I say, trying to give it back to him.

"Naw, I'll be okay." He lies to make me feel better. Besides, it's covered in Wolfie slobber."

"Quick, get some heavy rocks to hold it in place." He crawls around and brings back some clunky stones. While I stretch out the sweater as much as I can, then put the rocks on top, so they don't see it's a trap. We high-five, and Wolfie joins in by licking our faces.

"Onwards and upwards!" I cheer.

"What does that mean?" Matt asks, running beside me.

"It means let's get out of here and get some moon pie!"

CHAPTER 17

WHAT'S EATING YOU?

We're running and stumbling, trying to keep up with Wolfie.

"Wait, Wolfie! We only have two legs!" I shout through my labored breath. I charge ahead because I hear something behind me. Or maybe it's the Hellion up ahead. It's hard to tell with all the echoes. Just then, the Hellion rounds a corner and comes into view. It's approaching slowly and silently. We are about to hide when we see Celeste and Kyp hanging off the side of the beast. Celeste must be controlling it. Seeing it go slowly, it looks like a train disguised as a dragon.

"Quick, jump on!" yells Celeste, waving us over.

Matt and I run towards the gliding Hellion and try to coordinate running and climbing aboard the awkward monster train. Celeste is trying to slow it down as much as possible and extends her hand to pull us aboard. Matt and I are not the most graceful at this sort of thing, especially when we're messed up from being underground too long. We fumble to be first to jump on the step, and our feet get tangled up, making us both fall flat on our faces in the dirt. We push and pull at each other to get up and scramble to catch up to the moving Hellion.

As it goes around us, we notice it's on a thin uni-track, and it's heading towards the exit. Yay! Matt and

I high-five, then catch up to it and hop on the thin ledge at the bottom of its long silver neck. Celeste and Kyp pull us up the steps and into the belly of the beast. In the distant shaft behind, I see three burly goons running towards us, shouting and waving their tasers. Then they disappear with a shriek into the crevasse along with Matt's hoodie.

"Yippee-Ki-Yay! It worked." Matt yells, then high-fives everyone.

"Wow! That was a close one." I pant and lean over on my knees, "Celeste, we were captured! *Gasp*. The goon that grabbed us had horrible breath. Then we escaped from a dungeon with the key you gave me. *Pant*. Then my grandpa led me back to the pit, and Matt had to save me from falling into a crevasse. Now I owe him 100 moon pies." I stop to wheeze. "Oh, and there's no sign of Mikey. I don't think he's here." I look up at Celeste's confused face. "What happened to you guys?" I ask, panting.

Celeste stares at me and blinks, "You're right about Mikey. So, we rounded up the alien children, and then we had to tame the Hellion and . . . Wait, did you say your grandpa led you to the pit?" Celeste looks from me to Matt and back again.

"I swear, Celeste. My grandpa was talking to me, and he helped me and Matt find our way back to the pit and to you," I say, looking at all the puzzled faces around me.

"So, you're saying the radio wormhole is a portal to the afterworld, too?" Matt shudders.

"I never thought of it that way before, Matt. But yeah, I feel like in outer space, we're all connected on a different level. I feel closer to my grandpa."

Everyone looks confused, so I change the subject. "So this monster isn't a monster after all, but some kind of mining machine?" I look around the bullet train cab. "But how did you figure out it wasn't a dragon?"

"I slowed it down with my telepathy and I could see it had wheels," Celeste said, tucking her hair behind her ear. "It's a mine hauler shaped like a dragon. Its head holds the fire that drives the engine, and the grill has teeth like fangs," explains Celeste.

"It pulls cars behind it to carry the ore out of the mine. The cars look like a long tail to scare us," Kyp tells us. "There's so much smoke when it stops that you can't tell it's a train."

"You wouldn't want to look at it closely. It is scary looking, and the sound it makes is even scarier. It's like, 'Halloween' scary!" gasps Matt. "It's good that you guys could turn off the noise."

"The shoot on the side of its mouth must be like an excavator, where they feed it." I guess.

Kyp shows us the place where they empty their buckets. "Yes, and if we do not feed it enough, the claw arm is activated and throws us back to the pit with our buckets."

"Where are the kids now?" I ask, looking around. "Don't worry; they're safe inside the tail. I saw a big red button beside the door, and I used my telekinesis to push it, and the monster lay down and died," Celeste recalls. "Kyp and I climbed in and saw that it was just a train with all these half-empty carts in the back." Celeste pats Kyp on the shoulder. "We figured out how to dump all the ore that had been fed to the Hellion.

Then we showed the children that it was just a mine cart and could transport them out of the mine. They were so excited to jump in for a ride to the surface." Kyp and Celeste high-five.

"I asked them to be really quiet." Kyp peeks into the back of the monster. "I think they fell asleep."

"Kyp and I got bored waiting for you, so I taught him how to play tic-tac-toe. He's super good at it." Celeste shows me the charcoal and slate rock they used to play the Xs and Os game. "Then he taught me one of their games, 'Endiku'. I'm still learning, it's really complicated." They smile at each other. "Oh, then I found an old granola bar in my pocket, so we shared it. He loves our kind of chocolate."

"Shoq-lot! Ummmmm." Kyp closes his big yellow eyes and licks his thin lips.

"You guys were playing games and eating chocolate while Matt and I were imprisoned and lost in the 'tunnel of terror'?" I shake my head, confused at my angry feelings. Celeste doesn't notice.

"Yeah!" she says, looking at Kyp, "We discovered that we both think in pictures, and if we concentrate really hard we can see each other's pictures. It's so cool. That's how we communicate."

I look between them and realise that I feel a little jealous.

"Just forget it!" I say, feeling embarrassed. Celeste pulls out her worry stone and rubs it. "Let's focus on getting out of here so we can get back home."

"Hey where's Wolfie?" Matt interrupts our spat.

We all look around and realize that Wolfie is not on

board with us. "He was right behind us," I say, opening up the hatch of the beast. We see poor Wolfie running behind the Hellion with his tongue almost touching the ground.

"There he is! Slow this thing down, Celeste!" I yell as I reach out my hand towards Wolfie. But it's no use. He slows down, and the Hellion picks up speed.

"Nooooooooooooo!" I cry as Wolfie collapses on the dirt path and sadly watches us disappear.

CHAPTER 18

RACE YOU TO THE TOP

"I'm trying to slow it down," says Celeste, with her eyes closed and her hands on her temples. The Hellion shudders and shakes as it picks up speed. Matt reaches up and pulls down on the lever over his head, and the Hellion slows down and comes to a halt.

"Thanks, partner," I open the door. There's Wolfie, limping towards us.

"Come on, boy!" I yell, jumping off the steps and running to help my fur buddy. I look beyond him, and there are at least fifty angry, green goons, with tasers and sticks, running out of the passageway towards Wolfie . . . and us! It's no use. He won't make it. I almost reach him when Wolfie flies up into the air and over my head toward the Hellion. I stop in my tracks and watch as Wolfie soars to the open door and lands safely on the steps and in Kyp's arms. Celeste is looking out the door, smiling at them, and I'm thinking; Nice going, Celeste!

We make eye contact and her smile disappears, "Jump in, Hawk! We have to get out of here!" I look back at the goons, who stand there in shock because they've never seen a flying Wolfie before. But then they yell and lunge towards me.

"AAAAAAaaahh! Wait for me!" I cry as I bolt back to the unmoving train monster.

When I jump aboard, I find Matt and Celeste frantically trying to get the monster into hyper-speed.

"Why won't it work?!" Matt cries.

"I don't know! It worked before." Celeste pushes Matt out of the way and holds down the red button. "I think we broke it."

"Celeste, use your superpower to move it," I shout, noticing the goons are closing the distance between us.

"I tried, but it won't move!" she wails, "I don't know what's wrong." She points to the dashboard of lights, levers, and switches. I rush over to look at all the options. I push a button, and the Hellion shrieks. Wrong button! Then I think of something.

"Matt, release the handbrake. It's over your head!" I shout.

Matt yanks on the lever, and the Hellion immediately starts to move. *Phew!* We all breathe a sigh of relief and turn towards each other to do our secret club handshake. Suddenly, a goon jumps on the step and tries to open the Hellion door.

"AAAAAAaaahh!" I shriek when I see a hideously distorted alien face pressed against the hatch window. His nose and lips are an ugly smear, and his yellow eyes bulge out at us. He's about to swing his stick and break the window when Celeste changes gears and the Hellion goes into hyper-bullet-speed. The goon is sucked off the ledge with a surprised yelp.

We breathe a sigh of relief when we hear the screech of the Hellion. Now it sounds like freedom. We high-five each other, and even Wolfie gives us a high-paw while he cuddles with Kyp on the floor.

"Maybe you can show me Kyp's game later, Celeste?" I ask shyly, looking at her.

"Sure, Hawk. I'd love to beat you at 'Endiku'." She jokes, punching me lightly in the arm.

"Next stop, Hamelin," says Matt, pretending to be the train conductor. "Yippee-Ki-Yay!"

The Hellion rounds a corner and then starts to climb. We spiral upwards on our speeding train until we are all dizzy and falling over. "Oh, man! This is worse than the 'Gyro Rocket' at Wally-World," I moan. But I don't mind because we are flying towards the surface, and I can't get out of here fast enough. Everything is a blur, but as the Hellion slows down, we see where we are. The tunnel is getting narrower, and the opening is up ahead. The light at the end of the tunnel looks like fire. Our eyes got used to the darkness of the cave. The bullet train shoots through the opening, and we are all blinded by the light. "Aaahh!" The blazing sunshine burns our eyes and heats our skin as we try to make out what's happening. We're going too fast, "We're gonna crash!" I warn them.

"Cover your eyes!" Celeste yells as the Hellion comes to a grinding stop on the track. She blindly reaches up and grabs the eye shields for each of us from a hook by the door. Kyp then pushes the button to empty the Hellion of its cargo.

We are shaky after the light-speed trip to the surface.

Matt and I smile and click our rings together as we go outside in our cool alien shades. The breeze feels amazing on my face. I'm relieved to be out of that cave.

"C'mon guys, let's help the kids!" We rush to the back of the Hellion, where the poor child slaves are rolling around on the ground. They are in pain and confused because they've been underground for so long. Celeste hands out the eye shields and Kyp helps them put them on so they can adjust to the outside world again.

The little aliens are all wobbly, so we help them stand up and look around at the endless sky and beautiful landscape of colors. We fill our lungs with fresh mountain air and look out at the view. Their tri-sun is really bright—like three suns in one. It's awesome to see the outside world again. Long trails lead down to a nearby village and dots of other villages in the distance. Little alien dome-dwellings nestle among clearings of the blue and orange forest. The alien landscape is beautiful! We see crops of unknown grains growing in rows, orchards of weird cactus trees, and odd rock formations scattered about. We watch as Kyp and his friend Babu organize the children and help them traipse down the mountain toward the village and their waiting families.

"That must be Hamelin," I say wistfully, "You know we have to destroy the mine so the goons can't force them into slavery again. Can you use your power to collapse the mine, Celeste?" I ask.

"I don't think so, but I have a better idea," she says, walking towards the Hellion. "I thought we could take care of two things at once—if we crash the Silver Hellion into the back of the opening."

"Woohoo, you are a genius, Celeste!" says Matt, as she blushes and looks away.

"Let's wait a bit for the children to get far enough away so that it won't scare them. Then we can shoot this bullet train into the opening . . . like a bullet," I say, turning my head toward the trail, I see Kyp and Wolfie coming towards us.

"We have come to thank you and say goodbye, friends," Kyp ESPs. "It is like a dream. I am not sure if I will wake up tomorrow down in the mine." His big yellow eyes sparkle with tears. "But thank you for making my wishes come true—for all of us. We know that if we stand up for ourselves, miracles can happen. I will transcribe the events of today and about all of you so that we will never forget. It will be titled: *Superheroes from Planet Earth*." He reaches out with a stick and scratches two lines down and two across in the red ground. Then he hands the stick to Celeste telling her to go first. They alternate scratching Xs and Os on the grid until they run out and it's a tie game. They high-five and Kyp says he'll leave the game there as a souvenir.

"Say goodbye now, Wolfie."

"Wow. That's lit, Kyp. Wait, you changed his name?" I ask, petting Wolfie's soft muzzle.

"Yes, he told me he likes it better," Kyp ESPs, as he smiles down at the half-wolf, half-snow leopard who almost gave his life to save Kyp.

"Goodbye, Wolfie. I'm going to miss you," I tell him. He whines softly, and looks at me with his intelligent, knowing eyes, and gives me a deep stare that pierces my heart. I have a lump in my throat as I hug him and he puts his big furry head on my shoulder. He makes a deep howling singsong sound and I know he's going to miss me too.

Matt and Celeste kneel and give Wolfie a big hug, then we high-five Kyp.

"Hey, you can keep the dress . . . errr jersey. It looks great on you. Go Panthers!" says Matt, with a fist pump. Kyp hands him something and then runs down the yellow trail to catch up to his friends.

Matt shows us the tiny glass prism he holds in his hand.

CHAPTER 19

GOOD ENDINGS

point up at the yawning mouth of the cave and ask the obvious question, "How are we going to get the Hellion back up there and into that hole?"

"Easy, we just start it up, put it in reverse hyper-speed, and send it back up to crash the opening," Celeste says, walking around, checking the angles.

"But if the goons make their way up here, they could start things up again," I grumble.

"Not if we fill it with rocks first, so it's heavy. When it goes into hyper-speed, it will crash into the opening of the mine so hard it'll go right through to the other side. The top of the mountain will crash down and destroy the Hellion at the same time." Celeste looks at us so innocently as she says this that we can't help but smile at her.

"I like how you think, Celeste," says Matt. "Let's do this!" Matt picks up some rocks to carry over to the Hellion.

"That's okay, Matt!" Celeste says, "Allow me." She looks at the hill next to the Hellion, and suddenly a bunch of loose rocks shake, then roll down the grade. She starts a small avalanche of falling rocks and boulders that the excavator sucks up and fills all the carts, with dust flying everywhere. We watch as the hangry alien monster has one last meal and digests the rubble. *Sheesh! That is scary.*

"Okay. What now?" I ask Celeste since she's obviously thought out all the small details.

"We shoot it like a bullet into the hole, and it will go through the other side of the mountain because of the speed and weight," she says.

Catching onto the plan, I climb into the cabin, set the gear to full power reverse, and tell them, "It's all ready to go. We just need to push the red button to start it up and get out of the way."

I check to make sure the child slaves are at the bottom of the trail and heading for home before I nod to Celeste.

We run a safe distance away to avoid the flying wreckage of the train and collapsing mountain. Then Celeste puts her fingers up to start the countdown.

Three, two, one, blast-off!

Celeste uses her telekinesis to push the start button, and the Hellion jolts forward, shaking off excess rocks and gravel as it rolls. It makes a horrible shriek as it pops into gear and roars backwards in a blur. We didn't know what we were in for, but the angry Hellion hits a rock near the tunnel and derails flying off its uni-track. Airborne, it sails through the mine opening so hard that it crashes the far wall with a tremendous explosion. Then everything is quiet, like the calm before the storm.

We look at each other, and we're about to high-five when the mountain shudders and quakes. Big chunks of rock break off the hill and start to roll down towards us. The peak of the mountain trembles and sinks into the opening. It looks like a scoop of ice cream melting into a cone when warmed by a blowtorch. The mountain now has a flat top with the Hellion nose poking out of its mouth and a dragon tail dangling out behind. It's Monster Mountain—a disturbing reminder of what could happen if you go into the mine.

We nervously look at each other and then down toward the villages to see hundreds of aliens jumping up and down, clapping and cheering.

"I guess they're not mad about the mountain!" I say to Matt and Celeste.

There was only one thing left to do, and that was to get the 'radio' out of Matt's backpack, where he'd been carrying it this whole time, and go back home—just like Grandpa said.

Matt points at the collapsed mountain. "Wasn't the wormhole in there?"

Celeste rubs her worry stone inside her pocket "Oh no, we just destroyed it!"

"Wait, let's check the radio," I say, turning the radio over in my hands. "It says '*Scan*' here." I point to a small dial on the side. "Maybe it searches for wormholes?"

I turn the dial, and we hear a bit of static. I climb with the radio up the hill, and the static gets louder. I turn the dial a bit more, and the radio starts to glow green.

Celeste follows me. "I think we're getting warmer."

Matt runs ahead, up the hill. "Maybe we'll find it at the top."

As we climb, the static cuts in and out as it searches. The green glow gets brighter as we climb higher. I stumble toward the head of the Hellion and hear a low beeping sound.

"Quick, everyone, let's get back in the Hellion." I climb sideways into the tilting cab as the beeping gets louder, and the radio gets even brighter. "C'mon, get in!"

The green glow blinds us as we fumble around in the cab. The Hellion starts to shake and then lets out one last dying screech as I set the radio dial to E. We all put our hands on the glowing device, and I push the Transmit button. I hope we end up in my garage on planet Earth.

The last thing I hear is eerie music, like a flute, echoing from deep inside the mountain. Then whoosh! We spin like tops in zero gravity through a tunnel that stretches and shrinks, tilts and straightens as cool flames snake by us at light speed. Then complete darkness . . . again.

EPILOGUE

We come to my garage, surrounded by boxes, bicycles, and tools.

My dad really does need to clean out this place, I think to myself as I look over at Matt and Celeste, sprawled on top of some panels of plywood and siding.

"Come on, guys, wake up. Look, we made it! Let's go to the clubhouse." I drag myself up and help Matt and Celeste into the clubhouse, where we collapse on our orange couch. I've never been so happy to see this old couch before.

Knock, knock, knock!

We look at each other.

"Hey, Hawk. Can I come in?" The voice sounds familiar, but I can't tell who it is because my ears are still ringing.

"Who's there?" I ask.

"It's me, Mikey!"

Matt, Celeste, and I smile, then laugh, and do a happy dance right there in the clubhouse.

"Hold on one sec, Mikey!" I call out as we celebrate *not* disappearing Mikey.

I open the door, and he comes in looking very suspicious. He's even more surprised when I give him a big hug. Big Mikey's eyes go wide, and he shoots a questioning look over at Matt and Celeste.

"Whoa! What'd you do that for?" He says, turning bright red.

"Just happy to see you," I tell him, backing up so he can come in. "So, you didn't go into my garage . . . errr I mean, where did you go, man?" I ask him innocently.

"My mom called because Fred jumped out of his fishbowl. I had to go save him. But I did go in your garage, and I have a question."

Gulp! I look over at Matt and Celeste's worried faces.

When he sees our nervous looks, he says, "What? It's not like you have a time machine in there or something!" He laughs, shaking his head.

Mikey squeezes between Matt and Celeste on the couch and says, "I thought we could have a party in here with the basketball team. We can make more popcorn for our experiment and the team can help us decide which one is the best . . . for our science project."

We all look at each other and start laughing our heads off.

"Ya, sure! Sounds like fun. We could get some cola and milk too," I add.

"Blech! Cola and milk . . . together!" Mikey shrugs, "But first, you gotta fix that annoying clock radio in there. It beeps way too loud!"

Stay tuned to Black Hole Radio!

GLOSSARY OF SPACE AND SCIENCE TERMS

Black hole: A region of space where matter has collapsed in on itself.

Cave popcorn: Small bumps of calcite, aragonite or gypsum that form on surfaces in caves.

Claustrophobia: The fear of being enclosed in a small space or room and unable to escape.

Cosmic: Relating to the universe or cosmos.

Cosmologist: A scientist who studies the origin and evolution of the universe.

CPR: Stands for cardiopulmonary resuscitation. Used when someone's breathing or heartbeat has stopped.

Crevasse: Narrow opening or crack in the ground or a glacier.

ESP: Extra Sensory Perception. The ability to read each other's thoughts.

Exoplanets: Any planet that is not within our solar system.

Gravity: A force that pulls two objects toward each other.

Halitosis: Bad breath.

Hawking, Stephen: A 20-21st century cosmologist and theoretical physicist known for his work with black holes and relativity.

Hellion: A rough or rowdy person, a troublemaker.

Humanoid: A being that resembles a human in shape or character, especially in sci-fi.

Hyperspace Highway: An extra-dimension of space through which starships can travel faster across the galaxy.

Labyrinth: A place that has many confusing paths and passages, like a maze.

Light speed: The speed at which light travels (about 1.07 billion km per hour).

Mayday: Comes from the French expression "m'aider," meaning "help me".

Ore: A mineral which has valuable metal inside it, usually extracted from a mine.

Perseid meteor shower: This meteor shower takes its name from the Perseus constellation in the northern sky, where you can see them in August after sunset.

Portal: A gateway to another world of the past, present, or future.

Prism: A prism is a clear, triangular device that can refract light or bend and separating different colors within the light, creating a rainbow effect!

Spelunking: Visiting or exploring caves for fun. It is also called caving.

Stalactite: A form, like an icicle, found on the ceiling of a cave made by silty water flowing down but with the minerals remaining suspended but extending over time.

Stalagmite: A form like an upside-down icicle rising from the floor of a cave made by silty water droplets from the ceiling that land on the floor with minerals building up over time.

Taser: A weapon that uses electricity to shock and stun people or animals.

Telekinesis: The ability to move objects at a distance by mental power.

Telescope: An optical instrument to look at the stars, making them appear closer.

Underworld: From Greek mythology, a form of hell ruled by the god Hades.

Universe: All of time and space and its contents. It is made of millions of stars and planets and enormous clouds of gas, separated by a gigantic space.

Uranus: The seventh planet in order from the sun.

Wormhole: Passage through space, creating a shortcut through time and space.

AUTHOR'S NOTE

**Here on Planet Earth, about 1 million
children are working in mines today!*
Here are ten reasons why this is unacceptable:**

1. Mining is very dangerous for children under any circumstances. Mining can lead to serious injuries, and an unknown number of children lose their lives while mining every year.
2. Around the world, children ages 5-17 work in mines for as little as $2 per day.
3. Children can be found working in mines in Asia, Africa, Latin America, and Europe.
4. Work for child miners includes digging shafts, crushing rocks, carrying ore in gold mines, and digging, scraping, and lifting in salt mines.
5. Child miners face many health problems due to the nature of their work, including over-exertion, lung ailments, headaches, joint pain, hearing, and vision loss.
6. Child mining doesn't receive the attention it deserves because there are so many more child workers in agriculture (farming).
7. Children are often forced to work in the mines due to poverty.
8. Companies need to have more programs to free children from this kind of slavery.

9. People often buy diamonds, gold, and precious gems from sellers and don't think about the children who worked to produce the jewelry.
10. All children deserve the right to be children and go to school.

*Includes information taken from
<u>https://stopchildlabor.org/?p=3853</u> with permission.

YOU CAN TRY HAWK AND MIKEY'S "POPPING CORN" EXPERIMENT.

Hawk and Mikey discovered that corn pops when the water trapped inside the kernel gets hot and turns to steam, bursting the shell and creating popcorn. Here are some questions Hawk and Mikey asked for their experiment that maybe you can try to answer:

Do different kinds of corn have the same amount of water inside?

Do all brands of popping corn pop as well?

How come some popcorn is big and fluffy, and others are smaller and less tasty?

Does popping corn from the cupboard or the fridge pop better?

What if you soak the popping corn in water before you pop it?

Put these questions to the test by popping the corn using different methods. What differences do you observe, count, measure, or taste?

With the help of a parent, pop some corn on top of the stove in a large pot. Then pop some in the microwave in a large bag. Use a large pot and bag because a small amount of corn produces a big amount of popcorn!

YUM, this is one tasty science experiment.

Do you like your popcorn with or without butter?

ACKNOWLEDGMENTS

I am grateful to the people who helped make this book a reality. First and foremost, my supportive and creative husband, Terry Coderre. He always had the solution to the plot holes. Many thanks to my astute editor, Talya Pardo, who found the plot holes. Beta-readers, proofreaders and the whole team at DartFrog Books who helped me put this book together. My kids, who were very enthusiastic about this endeavor from the beginning. I love you: Justin, Sophie, and Kelly.

ABOUT THE AUTHOR

Ann Birdgenaw is a librarian in an elementary school and always wanted to write a book of her own. She was inspired to write this story by a strange beeping coming from a box in her garage. When COVID-19 hit Canada, and everyone was in quarantine or lockdown, she had lots of time to imagine being sucked through a wormhole to other planets and what wonderful things she might find there.

Ann lives in Montreal, Quebec, Canada, with her family and two morkies: Bilbo and Sheba.

Visit Ann at:
https://annbirdgenaw.wordpress.com/
https://www.goodreads.com/author/
show/21269547.Ann_Birdgenaw
https://www.facebook.com/
Author-Ann-Birdgenaw-109480387962145
https://www.amazon.ca/Ann-Birdgenaw/e/
B0918TCRRT/ref=dp_byline_cont_pop_book_1

@abirdgenaw on Twitter
@annbirdbooks on Instagram

ABOUT THE ILLUSTRATOR

E. M. Roberts is a passionate intellectual property designer and illustrator. He graduated from Dawson College, Illustration and Design program in Montreal, Quebec. Among his interests are character design, futuristic aesthetics, and sparkling water. He lives in Montreal with his wife and two children.

Visit Ellis at:
https://www.behance.net/EllisRoberts

Stay Tuned for Furilani, Book 5 in the Black Hole Radio Series!

Stay tuned for another fantastic episode of *Black Hole Radio —Furilani!*

Did one of the coolest girls in the school just talk to *them*? Hawk, Matt and Celeste are having a blast using their special powers to build their confidence and their popularity. They made the basketball championships and they're winning over the kids at school. Hawk has been reading his Grandpas' journals and learning how to control the black hole radio in his garage. Unfortunately, Matt's crystal from planet Labyrinthia reacts with the radio to send them on another wild adventure. This time to planet Furilani; a bustling spaceport planet, where intergalactic jet-setters and futuristic fashionistas use furry little creatures as living fashion accessories. Fuzzy belts, furry capes and fluffy scarves are a hit with the cosmic customers who line up to buy caged sploots in the alien marketplace. Hawk befriends one of these little 'sploots' and realises how intelligent and sweet they are. Can he and his friends teach this 'selfish society' a lesson in kindness and empathy towards other species? And will rapping Busta-Masta-Matt, be the newest sensation on planet Furilani?

"

"Black Hole Radio also sucks readers in and doesn't let go until the story ends. The vivid descriptions will keep kids and adults entertained. [It] fuels the imagination, while also imparting an important message. It seems that even advanced intelligent alien races can be bullies and even enslave those living on other planets. Friendship, peace, and acceptance are the themes in Black Hole Radio [and] to always follow your passion and believe in yourself." – Entrada Publishing Review

www.ingramcontent.com/pod-product-compliance
Lightning Source LLC
Chambersburg PA
CBHW051232210726

48290CB00003B/922